Danny the Caterpillar

Dawn Brookes

Illustrated by: Angela Simonovska

Coming Soon

Ava & Oliver's London Adventure

Danny the Caterpillar

Dawn Brookes

Illustrated by
Angela Simonovska

This book is a work of fiction
Copyright ©Dawn Brookes all rights reserved
Published by Oakwood Publishing
Paperback Edition 2018

ISBN: 978 1 9998575 2 3

To Susie who loves butterflies!

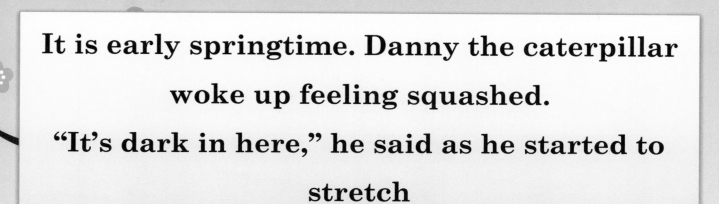

It is early springtime. Danny the caterpillar
woke up feeling squashed.

"It's dark in here," he said as he started to
stretch

Suddenly, his head popped out of the egg.

"Oooh, it's very bright out here," he said to himself. "I'm hungry!"

He found himself upside-down on a large leaf.

Danny started to eat the leaf.

Danny noticed a caterpillar on the leaf next door. "Hello," he said.

"Hello." The caterpillar replied, shyly.

"What's your name?" asked Danny

"Jilly," she answered.

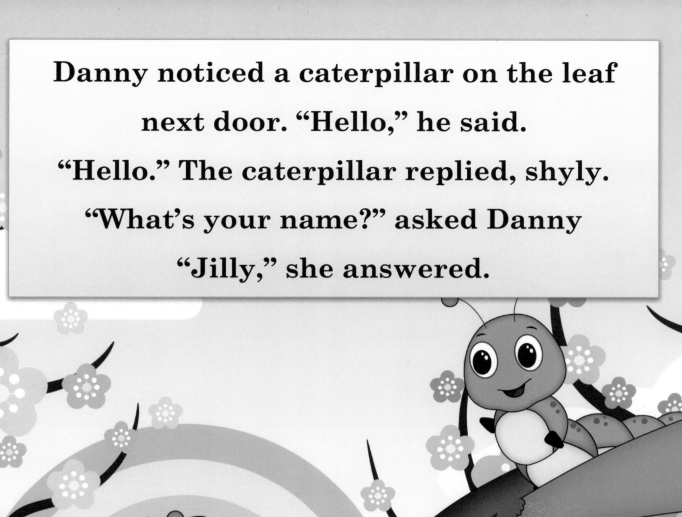

Danny started to show off and almost fell off his leaf!

Jilly laughed at Danny.

They both ate hungrily and created lace-like patterns on their leaves.

"I need to find another leaf," said Danny.

Suddenly, he saw a large shadow descending over Jilly.

"LOOK OUT!" he shouted and she managed to drop onto a leaf below, just in time.

It was a bird. The bird just missed landing on Jilly's head.

"That was close," said Danny. "You had better stay with me."

Danny and Jilly found lots of leaves to eat but the birds kept coming back looking for food.

"I have an idea," said Danny.

"One of us will keep watch while the other one eats," he suggested.

"That's a very good idea," said Jilly.

They managed to eat all day and were very pleased to rest that night. They were very happy!

The next day they woke up early.
"You look bigger," said Jilly.
"So do you!" remarked Danny.
"We are growing." Danny
felt his skin growing tighter AND tighter!

"What's happening?" asked Jilly, sounding frightened.
Danny saw that Jilly's outer skin was bursting but she was still a caterpillar, just bigger.

"It's alright." Danny explained.
"You have become too big for your boots- or should I say skin?"

Danny & Jilly ate all day long while avoiding birds that seemed to be very busy.

"Hello there," said a beetle, who walked along the branch above them.

"Hello," replied Danny. "Where are you going?"

"Here and there, looking for food," said the beetle as he went on his way.

Night-time came at last. "Look at that bright light in the sky," said Danny, as they watched the moon.

The next day they shed their skins again and became even bigger caterpillars.

"You look very nice," said Danny.

"Do you think?" asked Jilly, fluttering her eyelashes.

A bee buzzed overhead, searching for pollen.

"Who are you?" asked Danny

"I'm Buzz," replied the bee. "Sorry, can't stop, I'm a busy bee!"

Danny and Jilly ate and ate.

Every day they grew larger until they felt something strange happening.

"I think we need to move away from these leaves and find somewhere safe," said Danny.

They managed to avoid a spider's web while travelling.

They found a branch and hung upside-down.
Danny and Jilly didn't know what was
happening to them.
Their skin split for one last time but this time
they became very still.
They stopped being caterpillars. Danny &
Jilly were now pupae.

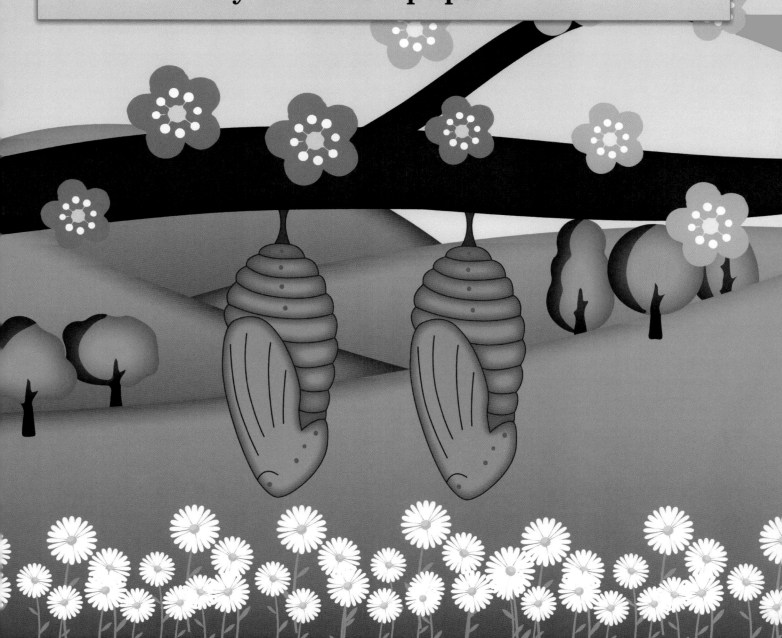

Birds flew past the branch searching for food.

Squirrels crossed over the branch collecting nuts.

Cats climbed onto the branch chasing birds!

Ladybirds landed on the branch.
Everything seemed normal from the outside
but a miracle was happening on the inside!

Early one morning, the outer cases of the pupae split open.

Danny came out first feeling exhausted and rested for a while. His body felt different.

He watched in amazement as Jilly made her way out of her casing.
"You're more beautiful than ever!" he exclaimed.

Danny stretched and fluttered his wings.
Jilly stretched her wings.

They had turned into butterflies.
Beautiful Red Admiral butterflies.

They flew away together to explore their new world.

Danny and Jilly enjoyed being able to fly among the flowers.

They saw more of the world and were very happy.

You might catch a glimpse of Danny, Jilly and some of their friends in your garden or in the countryside if you look very closely!

Dear Children

Springtime and Easter always remind me of the miracle of new life! I hope that you have enjoyed reading this book and that it makes you want to go outside and see all of the lovely creatures out there.

If you have enjoyed getting to know Danny the Caterpillar please ask you mum or dad to post an honest review on Amazon to let other readers know how much you liked it. I love hearing from children who have read my books and the reviews always put a smile on my face!

Other Children's books by Dawn Brookes

Ava & Oliver Adventure Series
Ava & Oliver's Bonfire Night Adventure
Ava & Oliver's Christmas Nativity Adventure

Books for Pre-school children
Boats & Ships A to Z

Miracles of Jesus Series
Jesus feeds a big crowd!
Jesus heals a man on a stretcher

Coming Soon
Ava & Oliver's London Adventure

Vistit the website:
www.dawnbrookespublishing.com
Follow us on Facebook:
https://www.facebook.com/dawnbrookespublishing/

Why I wrote Danny the Caterpillar

It had been a long winter and on a cold, Sunday afternoon I was fed up with the cold weather.

I found myself looking forward to springtime when flowers would start to appear, new life would be born in nature and the birds would sing happily in the garden. I also found myself thinking about Easter as that is an important part of the spring calendar.

As I was thinking about all of this on that cold Sunday I thought of caterpillars and how they turn into butterflies through the process of metamorphosis. This miracle always reminds me of the Easter miracle.

What do you love most about spring?